W9-BZX-308

9781585362882

My Mom's Wedding

DISCARD

Written by Eve Bunting and Illustrated by Lisa Papp

PUBLIC LIBRARY
EAST ORANGE, NEW JERSEY

E
jP
Bunting

Text Copyright © 2006 Eve Bunting
Illustration Copyright © 2006 Lisa Papp

All rights reserved. No part of this book may be reproduced in
any manner without the express written consent of the publisher,
except in the case of brief excerpts in critical reviews and articles.
All inquiries should be addressed to:

Sleeping Bear Press™

310 North Main Street, Suite 300
Chelsea, MI 48118
www.sleepingbearpress.com

THOMSON
★
GALE™

© 2006 Thomson Gale, a part of the Thomson Corporation.

Thomson, Star Logo and Sleeping Bear Press are trademarks
and Gale is a registered trademark used herein under license.

Printed and bound in China.

First Edition

10 9 8 7 6 5 4 3 2 1

Library of Congress Cataloging-in-Publication Data

Bunting, Eve, 1928-
My mom's wedding / written by Eve Bunting ; illustrated by Lisa Papp.
p. cm.
Summary: Seven-year-old Pinky has mixed feelings about
her divorced mother's wedding especially when she learns
that her beloved father will be an attending guest.
ISBN 1-58536-288-3
[1. Remarriage—Fiction. 2. Divorce—Fiction. 3. Weddings—Fiction.
4. Parent and child—Fiction.] I. Papp, Lisa, ill. II. Title.

PZ7.B91527Mym 2006
[Fic]—dc22
2006002203

16.95
1/17/07
NRN

b12464806

For Erin and Tory, my favorite junior bridesmaids.
E. Bunting

To beautiful families everywhere.
L.W. Papp

My mom is getting married to Jim.

Tomorrow.

Tonight we have a rehearsal.

I'm the ring bearer, which means I carry the two wedding rings on a velvet pillow. It's supposed to be a boy carrying the rings. But we don't have a boy. "Anyway, a girl is better," Jim says. "This girl!"

I like Jim. I'm just sorry he's not my daddy.

I practice walking up and down the aisle carrying the velvet pillow without the rings and trying not to laugh when Jim makes faces at me.

Tomorrow will be real. And my daddy will be here.

He's flying in from Dublin, Ireland. That's where he went to live after the divorce.

I haven't seen him since Christmas, but he calls me every Saturday and sends me cards with shamrocks and leprechauns on them.

When we were sitting around the kitchen table eating pizza last night, Grandma asked Mom, "Why is he coming to the wedding?" First Mom said, "Shh!" Then she said, "I've told you before, because we're friends. Because I invited him. And because of Pinky."

I'm Pinky.

I can't wait for tomorrow.

I think I won't sleep from being excited, but I do.

And then it's today.

The wedding is at eleven so at nine we go upstairs to get ready.

Last night I tried on my dress for Jim to see. He's not allowed to see Mom's dress before today, which is some kind of wedding rule.

I came down the stairs like a model. Except I was giggling.

"You look like the Little Mermaid," he told me and hugged me hard. He and I have been reading *The Little Mermaid* every night.

Sometimes I feel bad because I like Jim so much. Almost as much as I like my daddy.

Mom's bridesmaid, Libby, is a good hair fixer and when we're dressed she does our hair. Mine has flowers called Baby's Breath braided into it.

All around us our house seems to be cozying in, watching and happy.

I look at Mom. She is so beautiful. I bet my daddy will want to marry her all over again the minute he sees her.

Then I look in the mirror and I can't believe I'm me.

"Can Horace come over?" I ask. Horace is my best friend. He's seven, same as me, and he lives next door. I kind of want him to see me.

"How do I look?" I ask him.

"Okay," he says. "But you've got stuff in your hair."

"It's supposed to be like that," I tell him, and he rolls his eyes.

People are already crowding in front of the church.

I wave out of the window of our big, black car and I stretch my neck looking for my daddy.

Mom squeezes my hand and whispers, "He's probably already inside, Sweetie."

I'm going to see him soon.

We go into a little room that smells of chalk and candle wax. I sneeze just as the minister comes in.

"God bless," he says and then, "Ready ladies?"

Grandma takes out the wedding rings she's been keeping safely in her purse and ties them on to my pillow with little ribbon bows. Her hands are shaking.

Libby fixes Mom's veil and her spray of roses.

Mom takes a quivery breath. I'm quivery, too.

We go out to the church lobby. I can hear the organ playing inside.

And oh my gosh! There's my daddy, waiting.

He kisses Mom on the forehead. "I'm glad for you, Caro," he tells her.

"And look at you!" He smiles at me.

"I want to tell you a secret," I whisper.

He bends down.

"You could marry Mom again. I've got the rings."

My daddy puts a finger across my lips. "Stop it, Sweetie. Your mom and I are just friends now. 'Just friends' don't get married. She loves Jim, he loves her, and we all love you. Don't forget about me. But let yourself be happy for them, Pinky. I am."

" I . . . I . . ." I begin.

Grandma touches my arm. "Time for you to go, Pinky."

I'm double quivery now.

My daddy blows me a kiss and gives me a little push and I'm walking up the middle of the church toward Jim and his brother.

There are so many people. They're all looking at me. It's scary. It wasn't this scary last night. I see Horace McClurg with his parents. I see my piano teacher, Miss Collins.

There's a shiff, shiff, shiff behind me that I know is the sound of Libby's silver slippers, and then the organ music gets really loud.

"Here Comes the Bride."

That's the signal for Mom and Grandma.

Grandma is going to "give Mom away." Someone has to. That's another wedding rule.

Suddenly I pull the little ribbons free, lift the rings from the pillow and hold them hidden in my hand.

"The rings, please," the minister murmurs.

I'm hot all over.

Grandma and Libby are peering at the empty pillow.

Grandma hisses . . . "Pinky!"

I don't know what I want. But I know if they don't have the rings they can't get married. Still . . . they love each other a lot. Daddy had said that and he'd said, "Your mom and I are just friends now. 'Just friends' don't get married."

That has to be true because I wouldn't marry Horace McClurg if you paid me.

"Don't forget about me!" Daddy had said.

I'll never forget about my daddy. I look across at him and he's smiling, looking at Mom and Jim, and I can tell he's happy for them. He'd told me that, too. What is the matter with me? What am I doing?

I take a deep breath, step forward and hold out the rings on the palm of my hand.

Jim takes one. "Thank you," he says, and I think he knows how muddled up I am. It's funny, Grandma gave Mom away to Jim and now I'm giving her to him, too. And it's okay.

The rings are on their fingers.

The minister turns them to face all the people.

"May I present Mr. and Mrs. Jim Bollinger," he says.

There's a thunder of applause and Jim kisses Mom and then he lifts me and carries me, and the three of us go down the aisle together. I don't know if that's a wedding rule or not.

But I like it.

EAST ORANGE PUBLIC LIBRARY

3 2665 0035 7426 8

jP Bunting
Bunting, Eve, 1928-
My mom's wedding

2/07

DATE DUE

GAYLORD   #3523PI   Printed in USA

ELMWOOD BRANCH